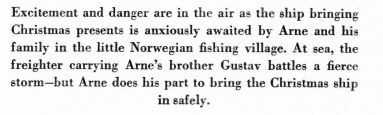
Excitement and danger are in the air as the ship bringing
Christmas presents is anxiously awaited by Arne and his
family in the little Norwegian fishing village. At sea, the
freighter carrying Arne's brother Gustav battles a fierce
storm—but Arne does his part to bring the Christmas ship
in safely.

Arne and the Christmas Star

Far out to sea, the freighter Stjerne *fought the storm bravely. At home in the little Norwegian fishing village, Arne and his family waited and prayed. It was the Christmas season, and the* Stjerne *was the Christmas ship this year, bearing Yuletide gifts and other good things for the village.*

But more important than the gifts, the Stjerne *carried her gallant crew — and Arne's brother Gustav, her first mate.*

How Arne does his part to help bring the Christmas ship safely into port makes a thrilling tale.

By the author of THE CHRISTMAS STOVE.

Arne
and the
Christmas Star

a story of Norway

Alta Halverson Seymour

illustrated by
Frank Nicholas

Follett Publishing Company
CHICAGO   NEW YORK

11777

Copyright © 1952, by Alta Halverson Seymour. All rights reserved. No part of this book may be reproduced in any form without written permission from the publisher. Manufactured in the United States of America. Published simultaneously in Canada by The Ryerson Press, Toronto.

Library of Congress Catalog Card Number: 52-14287

THIRD PRINTING

Follett Publishing Company
1010 West Washington Boulevard
Chicago, Illinois 60607

L 0560

Arne and the Christmas Star

To Todd
who was the first to make friends
with Arne

1

"OH, MOTHER, I hear Uncle Jens's folks are going up the mountain to the saeter tomorrow. Can I go along this time, do you suppose?" Arne's tongue was flying as he burst into the kitchen, and his blue eyes looked eagerly around for his mother.

No one was in sight but his grandmother, busy with her mixing bowl at the kitchen table. "Where's Mother, Besta?" he asked. "Cousin Bergel just told me they're going to take the cows and goats up the mountain tomorrow. Do you know who all are going? Do you suppose I can—"

"For goodness' sake, boy, you go on like a spinning wheel! It must be that red hair of yours that drives you along so fast. Just be quiet a minute, will you? I can only answer five or six questions at a time. Your mother and sister Margret are over helping Aunt Tina get things ready for the trip tomorrow."

"They're going, then! Oh, I hope I get to go too. I think I will, don't you?" Arne helped himself to a bit of cooky dough from the sticky yellow mass on his grandmother's floured board, looking warily at her out of the corner of his eye. Her hand was quick, and he might get a sharp rap on the knuckles.

But he didn't this time. She merely moved her board away from him and began adding flour to the dough. "Such a boy!" she exclaimed. "It would be a rest to me if your mother let you stay up on the mountain all summer."

Arne knew she didn't mean that. The two were the best of friends. Grandmother Dalen, whom everyone called Besta as a shortened form of the dignified Norwegian *bedstemor,* seemed to enjoy his tricks and teasing. She had even been heard to say, when she didn't know Arne was around, "I like naughty boys." Then she had caught sight of him and added briskly, "They give you something to work on."

Now she nipped off a piece of dough and molded it into a soft long roll which she deftly tied into a bowknot. She filled her pan with rows of similar bowknots and slipped it into the hot oven.

"Who's going, Besta, do you know?" asked Arne,

watching the cooky-making with interest but wishing
she would hurry and answer his questions. "I just wish
we had a saeter of our own."

"Lots of use your father would have for such a
thing!" scoffed Besta.

Arne's father was in the fish-packing business and owned just enough land to grow a little hay and keep a cow or two and some goats. But Uncle Jens was a real farmer; and, like most farmers in Norway, he had his own skyland pastures high in the mountain valleys where the grass grew green and lush. These were called saeters, and each had its little cabin where some of the daughters of the family spent their summers. The girls milked the cows and goats which were taken from the home farm to be pastured up there, made the cheese, and churned the butter. Arne thought some of the best fun of the summer was at the saeter. The day of moving up there was especially jolly.

"Cousin Signe will have to go, of course," he said, "and Bergel, I suppose."

"Yes, Bergel's old enough to help this year—almost as old as you. She's eleven now. Your sister Margret will take our own cows and goats up and tend to them. And of course Uncle Jens and Aunt Tina and little Knut will take the housekeeping things and help get the girls settled. And Cousin Evart—"

"And me—did they say I'm going?" Arne asked eagerly, as she paused.

Besta was something the shape of one of her own

butterballs, but that did not keep her from moving fast, or talking fast either, as a rule. Now, however, she seemed intent on her work, and when she answered she spoke almost reluctantly. "I haven't heard anything about your going, Arne. I did hear your father say he needed some extra help baling *lutfisk*. He said he was glad school is out so you can help."

"Baling *lutfisk*!" said Arne despairingly. He had done that before, plenty of times, especially when father had a shipment he wanted to get off in a hurry. "That's such a tiresome job, and so smelly! Do I have to stay home for that stuff?"

"You like *lutfisk* as well as anyone when it comes to the table," Besta reminded him. "Don't you know how good it is, with melted butter or nice milk gravy?"

Arne knew that well enough, but he certainly did not relish the idea of staying home from the first saeter trip of the summer to bale *lutfisk*. Part of the work connected with *lutfisk* was all right. It was fun to help unload the big cod from the fishing boats, to watch the men expertly split and clean the fish and spread them to dry. Ole Berg, the old fisherman who was father's right-hand man, had showed Arne how it was done, and even let him help.

11

Father thought Arne was a little young to handle the big, sharp knives, but Ole said the boy was very quick with his hands. So Herr Dalen gave his son a good Norwegian hunting knife with a silver handle shaped like a horse's head and a neat leather sheath which fitted on his belt. Arne was very proud of it and put it to good use under Ole's directions. But baling those bundles of dried fish was a very different matter. And certainly tomorrow was no day to spend on the packing-house dock at a tedious job like that. Then a hopeful thought struck him, and he asked, "Well, then, is Gustav going to help bale *lutfisk* too?"

His big brother Gustav was at home just now between voyages to sea—Gustav, who was going to be a ship's captain some day. He would sail as first mate the very next time the steamer *Laks* came to port here in Nordheim on its way up the fjord.

"What's that about Gustav?" called out a big voice; and a tall, dark-eyed young man with curly black hair came into the kitchen. "Oh, good for you, Besta! You're making *kringler!* Are those for the trip to the saeter?"

"Are you going to the saeter too, Gustav?" cried Arne accusingly. "And I have to stay home and bale smelly old *lutfisk!*"

12

Disappointment swept over him. It was worse than ever if Gustav was going and he couldn't. There was a lump in his throat, and it seemed to him he could hardly breathe. All spring he had been looking forward to this trip. He longed to be in the gay procession that would wind its way from the little village up the mountain road. Up it would go until the road became only a path, then still up and up. At last they would come to the little log house right on the cliff overlooking the fjord, with the pastures and valleys behind and mountains, gray with granite and green with pines, rising above it all.

First would go Suri, Uncle Jens's fat, light tan fjord pony with its black mane and tail. Arne was a great favorite of Suri's, for he always had a lump or two of sugar in his pocket, and she had learned to nuzzle for it as he patted and talked to her. Suri would pull the light hay cart piled with pots and kettles, milk pails and cans, churns and bedding, and all the other housekeeping things. When they reached the place where the road became no more than a trail, they would tether the pony and leave her to spend a pleasant day cropping tender mountain grass.

Aunt Tina would drive, and little Knut would ride beside her. The girls would be in charge of the cows and

13

goats. Uncle Jens and Evart and Gustav would carry big packs, because they couldn't burden fat little Suri too heavily. No horse-loving Norwegian would think of it.

There they would go, the bells on the pony's harness jingling, the cowbells ringing, little Knut tooting or whistling, everyone singing and laughing. Even his cousin Bergel, just a girl and almost a year younger than he was, would be in that jolly procession; and he couldn't go. This year it would be more fun than ever, for Gustav was going too, and there was always a special lot of fun where Gustav was. It seemed to Arne he would fairly burst with disappointment.

He had hard work to keep from crying, but of course you couldn't do that when you were twelve years old—especially when there were people around. But his nose pricked and his throat ached; he had to wink fast and turn and walk over to the sink as if he wanted a drink of water—which he didn't.

Gustav stood looking at Besta, and Besta stood looking back to him.

"You'll be going up later on in the summer, Arne," said Besta comfortingly.

"I don't care about going later," said Arne, and his voice came out something like a croak. "I want to go now, when Gustav's going, and everything getting ready—"

"I was thinking," said Gustav slowly. "They're going to need all the help they can get to carry the stuff from where we leave Suri. Arne's a pretty big boy now, and he could be a lot of help. I know that's one of the reasons they want me to go."

"They want you because everyone wants to have you around," said Arne, his voice still muffled. But the heavy feeling in his chest lightened a little, and he turned half around, looking hopefully at his brother. Gustav was pretty good at finding a way out of things.

Gustav said, "*Lutfisk* could be baled tonight as well as tomorrow. Father wants to have the shipment ready to send off day after tomorrow, that's all. We can work down there tonight. It's light on the dock till nearly midnight, these June nights."

"We?" Arne's grin began to break out. "Do you mean you're going to help?"

"Why not? I baled *lutfisk* when I was smaller than you are, and helped pack the kegs of pickled herring too, sampling as I packed. I used to kind of like to hang around that packing house. And it's fun to think of fish from the little port of Nordheim going all over, even as far as America. Come on, boy."

15

Arne dashed joyfully across the room. "Say, I like to hang around the warehouse, too, but I can do that any time, and the saeter—well, that's different. And this year Uncle Jens is going to rig up an extra good kind of special works to send the milk cans and hay from the top of the cliff down to the level land. We've been talking a lot about it. I want to help with that."

"Well, why not? You're pretty good at that kind of thing. Now we'll go down to the packing house, and I'll show you how to grab up those stiff old *lutfisk* and wind the wire around in a hurry. I've got a good technique. We'll work fast, and if we get enough done, maybe Father will let you go tomorrow."

The two brothers did not have very far to go, although their white house with its red roof and doors stood near the edge of the little harbor town far up on the Norwegian coast, where a mighty fjord joins the sea. They walked quickly along the narrow, cobbled street that twisted its way down to the wharf, past the brightly-painted houses—orange, green, and red—past the *stavkirke* with its roofs and gables rising one above another.

Arne liked that old church. He liked the carved dragon heads which sprung from the highest gables and rose above the small turret that topped the whole edifice.

"We're lucky to have it, you know," said Gustav. "There aren't many of those old churches around Norway, and none at all anywhere else. It's nearly a thousand years old; did you know that? It's lasted since the days the old Vikings used to have to carry spears or bows and arrows when they went to church."

"I like those old Vikings. And those were good days, Gustav," said Arne. "They didn't have to be sending *lutfisk* to America in those days."

Gustav laughed. "Well, we do. So shake a leg."

The packing house stood at the edge of the fjord, handy for unloading the fishing boats and for loading the ships that carried the kegs and cans and bales of fish to far-off ports.

Father was a little surprised to see them; and he was pleased, too, though he didn't say so. Usually he had to make it very clear when he expected Arne to report for duty. And here the boy had come down himself and offered to help. Here was Gustav, too, who was on a vacation and not expected to do real work.

Gustav did have a very quick way of handling that *lutfisk*. He picked up several of the long stiff pieces of fish which Arne thought looked exactly like pieces of wood.

17

These he arranged neatly in a bundle, bound it with wire, fastened and clipped it. As he worked, he sang some of the rollicking folk songs Besta had taught them long ago; and that made the job go even faster. Old Ole worked with them; he knew songs Arne had never heard. Before long Father joined the group; and by the time they stopped for supper, a good share of the work was out of the way.

"There, now," said Father with satisfaction. "We are going to see to it that those poor folks in America do not starve for good Norwegian *lutfisk*. Time to stop for supper. I wonder what Mother will have for us to eat."

"Hope it won't be *lutfisk*," said Arne fervently, and they all laughed.

When they entered the kitchen a few minutes later, they were pleased to see that Mother was cooking a large pan of meat balls.

Arne thought his mother was very pretty, with her coppery hair that shone like one of her own brightly-polished pots, her deep blue eyes and quick smile. And he knew very well she was the most comfortable person in the world to be around. There was a capable air about her that made one feel good inside.

His mouth watered as she filled a large platter with

meat balls while Margret set big mugs of milk on the table and Besta brought a large bowl of steaming hot potatoes. It was a favorite meal of Arne's, but for once he was the first to finish. He ran around the table to bow to his mother and father with the customary Norwegian, "*Tak for mad*," which meant, "Thank you for the meal." Then he said, "Now, let's get back to that *lutfisk*."

Father glanced at Mother, and his voice sounded as if he wanted to smile. But all he said was, "I'm afraid Arne is working himself out of a job."

Mother had been talking to Besta, and now she answered soberly, though her eyes twinkled. "It may be he will have to go along on that saeter trip and help there, if he's so eager to work."

Arne looked from one to the other. They sounded serious, but they often joked that way. He grinned and brought his hands together in a noisy clap. "Am I going to the saeter, then?"

"Let's see how we get along this evening with the work," was all Father would say. But Arne's heart felt light as he went back to the dock with the others. His fingers flew, and he sang louder than anyone.

2

T HE SUN was still high in that land of the midnight sun when Father said, "Past nine o'clock. Time for a boy to be in bed if he's to be up early to start for the saeter."

"Oh, Father! I can go?" cried Arne.

"Well, the *lutfisk's* nearly all baled. We don't want you around here tomorrow eating up all the pickled herring. Uncle Jens is going to need help. See that you give it to him."

"Oh, I will! Oh yes, sir!" cried Arne joyfully.

He wanted to say a special thank-you to Gustav for making it possible, but he didn't quite know how. Gustav was likely to make a joke of things, and this wasn't a joke at all. He did look up at his big brother, half shyly, as they walked up the hill toward home, and say, "I'm glad I am going. It was your doing, really."

"Oh that was just because I wanted you to carry

the heaviest loads," said Gustav, with a wink. "I plan to take it easy. Don't you loaf on the job, boy."

He smiled and gave a friendly yank at a lock of Arne's red hair, and the boy felt so happy he ran and jumped nearly all the way home.

It was still broad daylight when Arne tumbled into his feather bed and pulled another feather bed over him for covering. June nights grew cold along the fjord.

It seemed to him he had hardly fallen asleep when his sister Margret was calling, "Get up, lazybones, if you want to come with the rest of us."

Almost before Arne had finished his breakfast of mush and milk and cheese, he heard a clatter on the upper road behind the house and dashed out.

There they all came, just as he had pictured it. His cousin Bergel ran to meet him, her blue eyes shining. "Can you go, Arne?" she cried, and at his nod, "Oh, good! I like it lots better if you're along."

"So do I," said Arne, and they both laughed.

He adjusted his pack and fell in with Gustav and Uncle Jens and Evart. Margret, flushed and pretty, ran around trying to persuade their two cows and the goats to fall in with the others. Arne would have enjoyed helping her with that, but cows and goats were definitely

the province of womenfolk. He knew very well that
Margret didn't want any interference from him. Bergel
and Signe came to her aid; and soon the procession was
on its way, bells ringing, everyone singing and waving
and laughing, while Mother and Father and Besta called
out, "A pleasant trip!" "Good luck!" "God be with
you!"

The road ran at first along the foot of the mountain.
It was a good road, though there were fences across it in
many places, marking someone's land boundary. But each
fence had a gate which was opened to let the little caval-
cade through, and then carefully closed. Before long they
branched off to a road which climbed the mountain ever

more steeply and presently turned into a trail. Here they tethered fat little Suri, and the cart's load was divided among them. The men would have to make more than one trip down to get the rest of the goods.

Arne had been here many times before, and he rushed ahead so fast that Uncle Jens called him a mountain goat and told him not to fall into the fjord if he got to the saeter before the others.

They came at last to a log cabin with a sod roof. Pansies and bluebells were growing on the roof, and even a few little bushes and a tiny birch tree. The cabin stood in a wide clearing not far from the edge of the cliff

which overlooked the fjord. Little Knut had to be tethered to a tall fir tree for safety.

The older girls drove the cattle and goats into the pastures which sloped through the valley up toward the mountain.

Bergel wanted to go and gather wild flowers. "Come on, Arne," she urged. "There are foxgloves up here, and wild pansies and—"

"Oh, let's go fishing," Arne answered. "You can get wild flowers any time."

"That's right, do that," said Aunt Tina. "We could use some nice mountain trout. But first get in some wood, you two. It's high time for midmorning coffee."

"Evart, let's you and me get another load from the cart, and then go fishing with Bergel and Arne as soon as we've had coffee," said Gustav. "All right with you?"

"I'm always ready to go fishing," replied Evart, with a grin.

"I'll help get the load up; then I must get busy fixing our milk-can elevator," said Uncle Jens. "I've arranged with my neighbor to see to the end of it down at the bottom."

Arne was delighted to have the older boys in the fishing party. They were really experts, and he liked to watch them. Also they knew the best spots to fish. Up the trail a little way was a clear, deep stream, and there they soon got all the mountain trout they could use. Arne himself caught six, and Bergel four.

"Oh, I wish we could stay all summer," said Arne. "Don't you, Gustav?"

Gustav laughed. "This isn't man's work," he declared. "This is just fun."

"You're getting anxious to sail off," said Evart. "When do you go?"

"The *Laks* arrives in a few days. Then it will go up the fjord with me on it," said Gustav. He sounded happy at the prospect, but Arne's heart sank. He didn't like to think of Gustav going away again.

"Wish I could go," said Arne, with a gusty sigh. "I haven't even been on a boat and bicycle trip yet like some of the boys."

"You're too young," said Bergel in her practical way. "And you haven't a bicycle."

Gustav looked thoughtfully at his brother as they walked down to the cabin. "Could be we might take you along on one trip on the *Laks,* Arne. Put you to work, you know, swabbing the deck and peeling potatoes and all kinds of things."

25

"Oh, boy!" cried Arne. "Do you think I could, Gustav? And say, if you're going to be going up and down the fjord, you can touch home every now and then."

"That's just for a few trips," said Gustav. "Then I sail with Captain Olsen on the *Stjerne*. He says that will be the Christmas boat this year."

"Oh, good, the Christmas *Star!*" cried Bergel, for *Stjerne* is the Norwegian word for star. "That will be just right. It'll be fun to have you on the Christmas boat."

"First he goes clear to South America. Don't you, Gustav?" said Arne proudly.

"Yes, to South American ports and others too. We'll bring back meat and fruit and grain and unload a lot of it at Oslo. Then we'll take on more cargo—mostly Christmas things—and make the Christmas trip up the coast."

"And bring in toys and candies and fruit and nuts and gifts and everything nice," said Arne, his eyes glowing. "And you'll stay home for Christmas, won't you?"

"Yes, Captain Olsen says the Christmas crew should be home for Christmas. Nordheim is one of the last stops before Captain Olsen's home at Tromsö, where they'll put in for a couple of weeks or more. One of the other boys will take my place for that short pull."

"Everyone's going to be glad to see that Christmas boat come in," said Evart.

"And Mother'll be glad right now to see these fish come in," remarked Bergel.

Aunt Tina and the girls stopped their work of scrubbing every floor and wall and stick of furniture in the cabin to admire the morning's catch. Bergel stayed to help with the cleaning, and the boys went to help Uncle Jens, who was busy with wires and tools.

Uncle Jens had had a wire elevator before this for use in sending down milk cans and hay, but he felt it had been a somewhat makeshift affair. This year he wanted it to be strong and secure enough for any reasonable load, for his herd was an extra large one.

Arne liked this kind of a job, and he felt proud to be working with Uncle Jens and Gustav and Evart. Strong wires were fastened securely to trees and firmly anchored below to posts driven at some distance from the foot of the cliff. A milk can or a large bundle of hay could be sent down those wires in a rope sling, easily and swiftly.

When the little elevator was ready at last, Uncle Jens said they must send down a large milk can to make sure everything was all right. They filled one with water, tied it securely with a heavy rope, and watched as it slid and swayed its way down. Then the wires were tightened again, and they drew the milk can up and made more tests.

"I think it will do," Uncle Jens said at last.

With all the outdoor air and work, Arne was getting hungry again. So were the others, and every one was glad when Aunt Tina appeared with a large white coffeepot. "Time for afternoon coffee," she called.

Gustav sat where he could look out over the fjord, as if he hoped he might see the *Laks* coming in ahead of time. Suddenly he gave an exclamation and jerked his field glasses out of his pocket. "Some kid down there has turned over in a sailboat!" he exclaimed, jumping up and rushing to the cliff edge. The others followed.

"Don't believe that kid knows much about swimming," Gustav said, taking another quick look through his glasses. "He isn't making for shore—just trying to hang on to that capsized boat. That's slippery business. The water's deep and cold."

"It's Oscar Blessom's boat!" cried Arne. "But Oscar's on a bicycle trip. Must be Torger! He isn't very big, and I know he can't swim much. And there's no one near enough to see or help him." Arne looked at Gustav hopelessly. Not even Gustav could help now.

28

But Gustav's lips were set, and he went quickly toward the wire elevator.

"What are you going to do?" cried Margret anxiously.

"Go down the wires," said Gustav tersely.

"Oh, you can't! You can't do that!" protested Aunt Tina and the girls. "It isn't strong enough! It wasn't made for a man."

"Got to try it. Don't see any other way. Got to get there fast or it will be too late. Have you got some cloths, Aunt Tina? I have to wind them around my hands, or they'll be torn on the wires so I can't use them."

Aunt Tina flew for cloths and wound them quickly around his hands while Uncle Jens and Evart made a rope loop for Gustav to sit in.

All this was speedily accomplished. Uncle Jens and Evart helped adjust him in the loop while Arne watched, proud of Gustav, fearful he might get hurt, afraid he might not get there in time.

"Here I go," said Gustav. "Hold onto that rope, Uncle Jens, tight as you can."

The group at the top of the cliff watched breathlessly as Gustav went down. At first the wires swayed dangerously under his weight. Arne's heart seemed to come right up into his throat. Gustav was a good deal heavier than a full milk can. But he adjusted his weight to one side and another and then shot down swiftly.

The moment Gustav reached level ground, he jumped free of the rope. Torger must have lost his hold now. They could see that the boat had drifted away. Gustav knew that, too, for he was racing toward the water, pulling off his coat as he ran. He snatched off his shoes and plunged in.

Arne wished he had field glasses so that he could see every detail of what was going on. He could tell that Gustav was moving fast. But would he get there in time?

"He's making it," said Uncle Jens, his voice full of relief. "He's got hold of whoever it is. Bringing him in to shore."

"It's Torger Blessom, all right," said Arne. Gustav had the little boy on shore now. He laid him down on a large rock and bent over him, working quickly.

Arne looked at the wires and then at his uncle. Gustav could use some help down there. If they'd pull the rope right back up, maybe he could muster the courage to go down those wires as Gustav had done.

But to his relief, Uncle Jens said, "See, he has Torger on his feet. He'll be all right now."

"We must be thinking of getting started, now," said Aunt Tina. "We can't go down like Gustav. We have to take the long way around. I'll be up in a week or two, Signe, and give you a hand with making the cheese. And Bergel can help. She's eleven now, and it is time she learned."

Bergel smoothed her apron as they walked toward the cabin. She felt pleased and proud that Arne had heard her mother say this. He sometimes acted as if he

31

didn't think girls amounted to much. But she liked him and longed for his good opinion.

"Arne, you come again," said Bergel. "We'll go fishing."

"We'll be up, all of us, from time to time," said Aunt Tina, who loved the mountain saeter as much as anyone. It made her feel like a girl again to be up here, for in her younger days she too had had her turn at tending cows and goats on the mountain in summer, at caring for the milk and making the cheese. "Just for tonight I want to be the first to blow the saeter horn. Run and get it, Bergel."

Bergel ran into the house and came out with a long wooden horn, which she handed to her mother. The little girl longed to try it herself. They had told her, other summers, that she was too little; but perhaps if she was considered big enough to help with the cheese, she might be big enough to blow the horn, too.

She watched eagerly as her mother lifted it to her lips and blew a deep, mellow blast to call the cows home. Then, to her delight, her mother handed it to her and said, "You try it, Bergel. It will take more than one blast to bring the cows home."

Perhaps Bergel would have blown a good blast the

32

first time if Arne had not stood mimicking her, pretending with great effort to lift an imaginary horn to his lips, puffing out his cheeks, pursing his lips, and bringing out a small squeak.

Bergel had to laugh, and so did the others. But Margret gave her brother a brisk shake and told him to try to behave himself for once. "Try again, Bergel," she said. This time the little girl managed to bring out, if not as long and deep a blast as her mother had, at least a very creditable sound.

The girls would have to go out into the woods and valleys and up the mountainside to get some of the goats and even some of the cows, for the first few evenings at any rate. But before long, most of them would answer the call of the saeter horn.

The bells on the cows and goats were ringing over the valleys, and the saeter horn sounded again and again through the clear mountain air as they started down the path, Arne running ahead of everyone.

It had been a wonderful day, but he was glad to be going home. He wanted to hear all about the rescue of Torger Blossom, to see Torger himself and make sure he was all right. And he wanted very much to find out how Gustav felt going down those wires.

33

3

Gustav only laughed when Arne asked him how it felt to go down those wires. "You'll really have to try it yourself to find out," he said. "It wasn't much. Now you'd better run over and see Torger."

Torger was still a little pale and more than a little mortified over his accident. "Gustav said he'd give me a lesson in handling a boat," he told Arne. "He said maybe we could go out tomorrow, the three of us."

"If Gustav teaches you, believe me, you'll learn how," said Arne. "He's the one who taught me to sail and swim. Wonder why your brother Oscar didn't teach you."

"They are too near of an age," said Torger's mother. "Gustav is quite a bit older than you, and you are willing to learn from him. When Oscar tries to show Torger how to do something, it generally ends up in a fight."

The boys couldn't help grinning, for they knew Fru Blessom was right.

The next morning, Gustav took both boys out on the fjord. There was a stiff wind blowing, and the sailboat was not easy to manage. He said it would be good experience for Arne, and that if Torger learned in this wind, he'd never be afraid of a sailboat. Gustav was thorough in his instructions, and both boys worked manfully.

"I've got the hang of it now," Torger said confidently. "I bet I won't turn over in a boat again."

"I don't believe you will, Torger," said Gustav. "Now you two lads be sure to get out on the fjord and sail every chance you have. The best summer fun in the world is on a fjord."

"And the best thing to have fun with is a boat," said Arne.

"You're right about that," Gustav agreed heartily. Then he gave a sudden exclamation, "Put her hard over to the left, Arne! We're going in now as fast as we can! Do you see what's coming in from the sea? The *Laks* is almost in port."

Gustav sounded very happy, but Arne's heart felt heavy as he steered toward shore. It had been such fun to have his brother home, and the time had gone all too quickly. Now it would be months before he would be here for more than a short visit.

35

But Gustav wouldn't let anyone be gloomy today. No sooner had they tied the little sailboat up at the warehouse dock than he was rushing toward the big wharf, the younger boys beside him.

"From the way Arne's going, I'll have to hurry to get there first. He'll be going as first mate in my place, or maybe skipper," Gustav called out.

He stopped to smooth his hair and shake his coat into place before he talked to the captain. After that he hurried home to get his things, which were ready packed.

Besta and Mother came back with him, and Father, too, came down to the wharf to see him off. Half the town was gathering there, indeed, especially the boys and girls. They liked to watch the boat unload its cargo of mail and freight and take on other cargo to go up through the fjord.

Arne and Torger watched as a bright new spinning wheel was unloaded. "That's for my grandmother," said Torger, "and about time, too. She's been complaining that she wouldn't have wool ready for the Christmas knitting if that wheel didn't come soon."

Crates of oranges from America were next, boxes of groceries and drygoods, and windows for the new house going up at the edge of town. There was not very much to load on the boat here. The fish from the packing house went to ports farther away. Towns along the fjord could catch their own fish. There was mail to go. A few passengers got on. Arne saw a group of boys on board with sleeping bags and rucksacks. He knew their bicycles were stowed away somewhere and that they were on a holiday jaunt up the fjords and over the mountains. One of these days he'd be going on such a jaunt, too.

A little flutter of interest in the crowd made him turn quickly. To his surprise, he saw Uncle Jens coming down the street, leading Suri. He went straight over to the captain and said, "I want to send Suri up to Blegen for a little while. My wife's brother needs an extra pony to help with some farm work, and I can spare Suri just now. So can you take her aboard and make her comfortable?"

"*Ja, Ja,* certainly we can take care of Suri," the captain assured him.

But Suri did not seem to care for such a trip in the least. A broad band was securely fastened around her and a derrick swung over to lift her aboard. But little Suri stamped and champed and lifted her head, her eyes rolling in fright as she complained in loud whinnies.

No one thought of such a thing as trying to force the little mare aboard. Uncle Jens talked to her, and she quieted down a bit; but when the derrick came toward her again, once more she backed and stamped and whinnied nervously.

The other loading was finished. The sailors were closing the holds. But the *Laks* could not weigh anchor because little Suri, in spite of all wheedling, was flatly refusing to go aboard.

Arne only wished he had the chance Suri was refusing, but nevertheless he felt very sorry for the frightened little horse. Perhaps he could coax her a bit—he had done it often enough before.

He went over to try, fishing in his pockets as he went. Yes, there were two lumps of sugar. He put an arm over Suri's neck and offered her one, talking to her softly the while. She nuzzled her soft brown nose into his hand and seemed to feel comforted.

"Go on, Arne," Uncle Jens encouraged him. "She seems to listen to you."

So Arne stood there, coaxing little Suri, feeding her sugar, talking to her, patting her, until she stopped trembling and champing and at last let him fasten the big hook in the band which was fastened firmly about her. Then he ran onto the boat and stood there talking to her from the deck. Now at last she let them swing her aboard, and though she stamped anxiously at first, she allowed Arne to take the band off and lead her down into the hold.

"Wish I could go along with you, Suri," he said, putting his cheek against her neck and giving her a pat.

Gustav had come down to see that everything was in good order, and now he gave his young brother an en-

couraging nod. "That was a pretty good job, Arne; you saved the skipper a lot of time, and that may turn out to be a good thing."

"Do you think he might let me go on the boat some time, Gustav?" asked Arne eagerly.

"I can't promise a thing yet. You skip ashore now, and we'll see. The ship's bell is ringing. They want to get started. And our captain wouldn't care for a stowaway aboard, I know that."

So it came about that Arne was laughing as he ran down the gangplank just as they were about to pull it up. And instead of feeling sad as the boat steamed away with Gustav aboard, he was thinking of the day when he might be aboard too.

He looked up to see his father standing there, smiling down at him. "I thought for a minute there I was going to have two sons on that ship this time," he said. "Looked to me as if the captain could find a use for you."

"Oh, I wish I could be aboard, especially when the *Stjerne* sails out," said Arne, heaving a great sigh. "That's the life, isn't it, Father?"

His father laughed, a contented, good-natured laugh. "That's the natural way for a Norwegian boy to feel, I guess. I did my share of sailing, too, in my early days. But I understand there's such a thing as school. I hear boys are expected to go to that in Norway."

Arne knew his father was joking; so he smiled back, though school never seemed to him a very good subject for a joke. "I suppose so," he said. "But I like outdoor things so much better than schoolwork. I just wish it were summer all the year around."

Arne was not the only one who wished it were summer all the year around. Up at the saeter, the girls were having a merry time in spite of the work of caring for the cows and goats, milking and making cheese. There were berry-picking excursions through the woods and valleys to gather blueberries, raspberries, and the lovely bright *multer* berries which grew thick and red on their low bushes. There were visits with girls in neighboring saeters and fishing trips up the mountain.

"Don't forget I'm to learn to make cheese," Bergel reminded Signe one day.

"Oh, yes. Mother wouldn't like it a bit if we didn't get that tended to. We'll start with *gammelost*. That's best, anyway."

Under Signe's direction, Bergel warmed the milk and let it stand until the curds and whey could be separated. Then she dried the curds, crumbling them carefully with her hand, and set it all aside to ripen. Signe even let her add the caraway seed and salt.

When it was brought out some days later for inspection, Margret looked at it with approval. "We should save that for company," she said, sniffing with appreciation.

Bergel nodded, looking very grown-up as she tasted it with a businesslike air and added a little more salt. Then she put it away in a covered jar to ripen further. "I hope the company will be Arne and Evart and some of the other boys," she said, and though the other girls laughed, they agreed with her.

Down in the town, Arne was keeping busy, too. He had jobs of many kinds at home, running errands and getting in the wood for the old cookstove Besta preferred to Mother's new electric range. And he had to help Besta cut the hay in the little patch of ground that sloped from their house up the mountain. It was fun to get in there with a scythe, and to help Besta and Mother hang the hay over the wooden hay fences to dry before it could mildew on the damp ground.

He helped around the packing house, too. There were errands there as well as at home, and there was cleaning to do, and packing. Sometimes he was allowed to go out with the fishermen. He especially liked to go with Ole to fish for *torsk* and herring and halibut. Sometimes they took a rowboat or a small sailboat up the fjord. Sometimes they took Ole's big boat and went out to sea.

There was time for play, too, in the summer afternoons and long, light evenings. More than once Arne went away on a day's jaunt with Oscar and Torger and half a dozen other boys. They sailed and swam and fished on the fjord, and took long hikes up and down the fjord path and up the mountainside.

But Arne never let any of his activities keep him from being right on the dock when the *Laks* was due. Each time he hoped to hear the glad news that he was to be on board when the ship weighed anchor. Each time he asked Gustav eagerly if he was to go on this trip.

When two or three weeks went by with no invitation for Arne, he began to lose hope. But then one day Gustav jumped off the gangplank calling out, "Where's that Arne? You better go get some packing done, boy."

"Really, Gustav? Do I go this time?" cried Arne.

"Looks that way," answered Gustav. "The skipper says we're bringing Suri back this trip, and you'd be a good one to have aboard to help with that."

Arne gave a big, "Oh!" on a deep, blissful sigh, and

43

was off up the hill like a shot to tell Mother the good news and to see to that all-important packing. He had a lot of things he wanted to take, and he had a feeling Mother wouldn't think half of them were necessary.

"We'll be here for a couple of hours, at least," Gustav called after him. "Tell Mother to put the coffeepot on."

Arne loved that journey up and down the fjord, stopping at each small village with mail and freight. There were a few passengers, and he liked to see them get off amid the joyful greetings of their friends. Often they were met by a light boat which would take them aboard and then skim swiftly and quietly off to some town across the fjord or to some nearby farm.

He made friends with a little party of English lads who had bicycles on board and planned to leave the boat at the head of the fjord and go off through the valleys and over the mountains which Arne taught them to call by the Norwegian name of *fjelds*. He wished he had a sleeping bag like theirs and that he could sleep out with them on deck, though they told him it got pretty cold.

They let him share some of the meals they cooked over their tiny portable stove, and Gustav saw to it that he contributed fish balls or cheese or some other delicacy.

On the afternoon the *Laks* neared the head of the fjord, Gustav was at the wheel and Arne stood near him, watching the waterfalls dash violently down the high, steep mountain walls.

Suddenly he gave a shout, "Gustav, look out! Rocks falling! Big ones! Right ahead!"

Gustav gave one quick look, and his face was grim. Arne's heart beat fast. He knew it would be terribly dangerous to hit those rocks here where the *Laks* steamed between sheer mountain walls. But he saw that his brother wasn't losing his head for a moment. He was proud of the resolute look on Gustav's white face, the sure, firm way he managed to turn the wheel and guide the boat to avoid the rocks.

The captain came running up, his face as pale as Gustav's. "Good work, Gustav," was all he said, but his relief was plain to see.

At the head of the fjord, the English boys left them, though they stayed on the dock to watch little Suri taken aboard.

Arne kept a sharp lookout for falling rocks as they steamed homeward between the steep rocky cliffs. He was glad when they came to the places where the country flattened out a bit and there was room for a small village

45

or a few farms at the foot of the mountain. Often he caught a glimpse of a saeter high above them.

"Do you think we're going to get up to the saeter again this summer?" he asked Gustav, after one such glimpse. "I know the girls are counting on it."

"I'll have two or three days between my last trip on the *Laks* and the time the *Stjerne* sails," said Gustav. "That will be early in August. Let's go then."

"Shall I make a trip up and tell the girls?" asked Arne eagerly. "They'll have a lot of getting ready to do—a lot of baking and things."

"You hope," said Gustav, laughing. "Well, I hope so too, Arne. So we'll figure out the time and you can hike up that mountain and tell them about it."

Arne had made many pleasant journeys to the saeter, but there had never been one as gay as the trip up there with Gustav and Evart and a dozen other lads.

"Look! Look what the girls are using for pasture!" cried Arne, as they came in sight of the saeter. A shout of laughter went up, for Bergel had tethered a small white kid to the tiny birch tree on the roof of the cabin.

The shout brought out the girls, gay in their special holiday dresses. Arne thought they looked very pretty in their full, striped skirts with crisp, lace-trimmed white aprons and bright laced bodices over white blouses. A hand-made silver brooch fastened each blouse at the throat. Margret's brooch was handed down to her by

Besta, Arne knew; and he thought it was the prettiest one of all. These brooches were treasured possessions in Norwegian families.

Signe and Margret and Bergel had invited girls from neighboring saeters, and a good thing, too, for Gustav had brought his accordion and Evart his fiddle. There was dancing and singing and laughter under the trees. Arne and Bergel joined in the fun, for they could do the old folk dances as well as any of them.

Then a feast was spread out on the long table — fish and cheese and *lefse* and big bowls of berries with whipped cream, and *kringler* and cakes and cookies of all kinds. Bergel's *gammelost* was praised enough to make the young cheesemaker very proud.

The fun stopped toward evening, but only long enough for the girls to get in the cows and goats and do their milking, to make fresh coffee and replenish the dishes on the table. Then the dancing started again and went on far into the long summer evening.

At last the party from the village started down the trail for home, reluctantly, to be sure, but singing and laughing nevertheless.

It was a sleepy Arne who tumbled into his feather bed at last. This had been a long day, but a wonderful one.

4

THE *Stjerne* came into port a few days later, and
Gustav sailed away as first mate. He was so happy about
it that Arne couldn't help feeling some of that happiness
too. He remembered what fun it had been to go up the
fjord on the *Laks,* and he didn't blame anyone for want-
ing to go to sea.

But Gustav was sailing far away this time, all the
way to South America, touching at many ports on the
voyage. It would be a long time before he returned.

"Oh, Gustav!" The words fairly burst from Arne as
he stood watching the final packing. "I wish South America wasn't so far away!"

Perhaps Gustav knew how he would have felt if he
had been in Arne's place. He put his arm around Arne's
shoulder and said, "Look here, fellow, I've got something
I want to leave with you. Father gave me new field glasses
as a parting gift. I want you to have my old ones."

"For keeps?" cried Arne. It would be wonderful to have those glasses.

"For keeps," said Gustav, and was fully rewarded by Arne's shining face.

"Now you can watch us till we get clear out to sea and turn down the channel between the shore and the islands. In fact, if you go up on the cliff, you can watch us farther than that."

"Oh, I will! Oh, Gustav! And I'll be watching when the time comes for you to come home, too, you can bet on that."

The gift took most of the sadness out of the parting, though Gustav would be gone now until December when the *Stjerne* would come in with its load of Christmas goods. Then he would be home all through the holidays. That was something to look forward to.

The rest of the summer slipped quickly away. It was time for the girls to come home from the saeter, and Arne went with Uncle Jens and the others to help bring down the girls and the gear, the cows and the calves, the goats and the kids and the cheeses.

School was to start the next week, and he felt a little dismal about it as he talked it over with Bergel. "I hear that new teacher is very strict—Herr Professor Engstrand. Oscar said Pastor Beckstrom's son told him so."

Bergel nodded. "I heard so, too. But maybe we have to expect that, now that we're going to be in the upper room. Just think, Arne. We'll start learning English, and do a lot of things we couldn't do before." Bergel, very quick at her lessons, was in the same grade as her cousin.

"I'll like being in the same room with Nels and Oscar and those boys instead of a lot of little kids," Arne admitted.

"Yes, I think it's wonderful we're going to be in with the upper grades. And a man teacher. Makes me feel pretty grown-up."

Arne was surprised when he entered school that first morning and got his first glimpse of Herr Professor Engstrand. Somehow, from Oscar's remarks, he had expected to see an elderly gentleman. Herr Professor didn't look much older than Gustav. But he certainly was not like Gustav in any other way. There was no laughter in those stern gray eyes, and his mouth, straight and firm, didn't look as if it ever even smiled. He stood stiffly beside his desk, his shoulders squared.

When the school was assembled, he made a short speech. "I am new here," he said, "but we shall soon get to know one another. If you do your work well, we shall

51

get along without trouble. I shall put up with no laziness, no disobedience. You are old enough to know how to work, and that is exactly what I expect you to do." His words were clipped and curt, and Arne was sure you could have heard a pin drop in that quiet room. Lessons were assigned and classes were held in the most methodical order. Any lack of attention, any slightest sign of disorder, was promptly reprimanded or punished more severely.

Arne very soon made up his mind about one thing. He would try to obey orders to the letter. He could see there would be trouble ahead if he did anything else. He didn't know, of course, that this was Herr Professor Engstrand's first school and that he was desperately anxious to make a good job of it.

Winter set in early, and it was always a relief to Arne to get out of school. He liked to get his skis and go flying down the steep slopes behind the town with Nels and Oscar and Torger and some of the other boys. Evart was away at school this year, and sometimes Arne took Bergel with him coasting. She knew how to steer the long sled almost as well as he did.

He would stop at home in the kitchen first, for he was sure to find Mother and Besta having a cup of afternoon coffee. Sometimes Aunt Tina would be there, too, and Signe and Margret. Sometimes one of the neighbors would come in. But whether there was company or not, there was sure to be something good to go with the coffee— slices from a big, round loaf of ryebread with *gjetost,* Besta's special goats' milk cheese, or coffeecake, or *bakkelse*—crisp, delicious little cakes fried in deep fat, or some other of their many specialties. Mother and Besta were as good cooks as you'd find in all Norway, Father often said; and he added that that was saying a lot, for Norway was famous for its good cooks.

Sometimes as he came in, after skiing or skating or coasting, he would hear Besta's spinning wheel whirring comfortably away. She liked to spin the wool for her knitting and weaving. Even Margret, up-to-date as she considered herself, preferred the soft wool her grandmother spun to any other. Besta never looked as contented as when her foot was on that treadle, her practiced hand drawing out the fine strong woolen yarn.

Arne usually came from school with a rush and a bang. But one day he came into the kitchen without saying a word. Bergel was with him, and she too was quiet.

"Fresh *lefse,* Arne," said his mother.

Arne nodded, but for once he didn't make a move to take any.

Besta looked at him keenly. "Trouble in school, Arne?" she asked.

Arne's face darkened, and he doubled up his fists. "That Herr Professor!" he exclaimed. "He's just so mean and unreasonable. All I did was to ask Sigurd, just behind me, how far we were to study. And I had to stand up in front of the whole room for an hour." He flushed as he thought of it.

54

"Perhaps he thought you would have known how far to study if you had been paying attention," said Mother, shaking her head, though she felt sorry for Arne.

"Well, I was thinking of something more important than English grammar." In spite of himself, Arne's face lighted a little. For right in the midst of class, he had suddenly thought of a delightful plan—a surprise for everyone for Christmas. Mother was exactly right, though he didn't like to admit it. He had been thinking out details of his project instead of paying attention.

"How do you get along with Herr Professor, Bergel?" asked Besta.

"Oh, of course she gets along fine!" exploded Arne. "She always has her lessons, and she behaves like a little lady." The mincing tone he assumed almost made Mother and Besta smile, though they realized very well that this was no laughing matter. "Herr Professor likes Bergel, but he sure doesn't like me. I might just as well stop trying to please him."

"Oh, don't do that, Arne," urged Bergel. "You'll get used to him. And he does know a lot." She wished from the bottom of her heart that Herr Professor would say "well done" to Arne once in a while. He did do well in his history and arithmetic.

"Well, have some *lefse* and some *ost* and try harder tomorrow," said his mother sensibly. "You'll get along all right if you pay attention and study."

Arne took the *lefse,* but it didn't taste as good as usual. It didn't seem to him he could ever learn to get along with Herr Professor Engstrand. It certainly looked as if he were headed for trouble. And with Christmas coming, too.

But he did make an effort, and school went better for some time.

Bergel mentioned it with pleasure as they walked home one afternoon. "You're really doing fine in school, Arne," she said. "You haven't been in a bit of trouble lately. Herr Professor hasn't even had to look your way. I bet you could be right up at the head of the class if you'd try."

"There are so many things I like to do better than to have my nose in a book," said Arne carelessly. "I like to work out in the workshop for one thing. Right now," he added, his face brightening, "I'm working on—" Then he broke off abruptly and laughed. "Can't tell you what —it's a surprise."

"Oh, go on, tell me," coaxed Bergel, but Arne only shook his head mysteriously.

"You'll see," was all he would say. "I'd better be getting home to get at it. There's a lot left to do if I'm going to have it ready in time."

From early November, Arne had been spending every moment he could spare in the little workshop out in back. He was making a number of small ships, some with tiny sails, some with little oars, sawing and cutting and gluing and painting with great care. They would be hung all over the tree—red and green and yellow and blue.

There was to be at least one special one for each member of the family — a fishing boat for Father, the tiniest sailboat for Margret, a red rowboat for Besta, and a blue one for Mother. There should be one for each of the cousins, too, and Uncle Jens and Aunt Tina. And he wanted to make several for Gustav.

No one else in Nordheim or probably anywhere else would have a tree trimmed like that. It would be a surprise for everyone. Arne almost chuckled aloud whenever he thought of it.

His face was bright today as he ran into the kitchen. There were Mother and Besta, having their afternoon cup of coffee. The kitchen was filled with the good smell of baking. *Rosettes* were spread out on the table—delicate, beautifully-shaped cakes fried in deep fat. There were also crisp star-shaped cinnamon cookies.

He pulled off his cap and asked eagerly, "Any broken pieces for me?" He knew all the well-shaped cakes and cookies would be put away carefully for Christmas.

"Besta broke a few for you," said his mother, with a twinkle. "And before you go out to that workshop, get me some soap from the storeroom. I am going to take down the curtains and put them to soak."

For weeks, now, the house had been in a bustle and flurry of Christmas cleaning. Every spot was shining— floors and furniture, brass and copper. The house fairly seemed to twinkle.

He couldn't see why they had to take down the lace-trimmed window curtains to be washed and stiffly starched. Those curtains looked white as snow to him. But when he said that to Mother, she laughed out loud. "Not have clean curtains for Christmas!" she exclaimed. "What a boy you are, Arne! If your mother did such a thing, *Julenissen* would be so horrified he would run right away from our house."

Arne laughed, too. You certainly wouldn't want to scare away *Julenissen,* the little elf with the pointed red cap and little red suit. He was supposed to live in the attic and bring special good luck at Christmas time, particularly if one always remembered to set out his bowl of milk and give him his Christmas rice porridge. Arne had never actually seen *Julenissen,* but he knew someone in the family always saw to that milk and the porridge.

"*Julenissen* hates dirt," said Besta.

"I guess he'll never get scared away from our house, then," said Arne. "And I should think he'd like the Christmas baking even better than the cleaning."

"If he doesn't, I know somebody else who does," chuckled his mother.

Arne knew there would be stacks of *flatbrod,* hard and crisp and round, each piece larger than a plate. Besta baked these right on top of her well-scrubbed cookstove. There would be heart-shaped waffles, and *lefse* and *bakkelse* and *rosettes* and all kinds of good coffeecakes. His mouth watered at the thought. If a boy hung around the kitchen at the right times, he was sure to come in for a good many samples, especially broken bits.

He knew there would also be a final scouring of the house just before Christmas, that the windows and the copper flowerpots on the window sills would be gleaming. The geraniums and begonias would be coaxed into bloom for Christmas.

And of course the womenfolk would be busy planning and preparing food to last through the Christmas season, for no one wanted to do much work during the two weeks of the holidays. And there would be a great deal of company.

Father would see to it that they had all the best kinds of fish—the smoked and pickled herring. And the *lutfisk* —which he had so disliked to bale in the summer—would be a favorite part of the Christmas feasting. There would be cheeses, too, of many kinds, and pickled pigs' feet and headcheese, roasted meats and sausages. Mother always set out a good *koltbord*— a table laden with all these good things and many others; people could help themselves to suit their tastes.

Arne thought of all this as he fortified himself with a substantial snack. Then he went out to the workshop. He had almost enough little ships now, ready for sandpapering and painting. His worries about school were forgotten, and the time flew as he worked, his lips puckered in a low, contented whistle.

Suddenly he straightened with a start. It certainly couldn't be supper time yet. But Margret was coming down the path calling him.

"Don't come in! Don't come in!" he shouted, throwing an old blanket over his work. Then he ran out and closed the door behind him.

"I wouldn't come in, Arne. You know that," she said. Her voice sounded muffled and unnatural. In the light which streamed from the kitchen window, he could see that her face looked as if she were trying not to cry.

"What is it? What is it, Margret?" he asked anxiously. "Is something wrong?"

"We heard something over the radio," said Margret; and now, in spite of her efforts, her voice broke into a sob. "Oh, Arne, there are storms at sea—bad ones—sleet storms and ice storms right where the *Stjerne* must be now!"

Arne's heart seemed to turn right over. He knew very well the danger his brother was in. All his life he had heard of those winter storms at sea. He wished with all his might that Gustav's ship was safe right here in Nordheim harbor.

5

A VERY QUIET FAMILY gathered around the supper table that evening. Even the thought of his little ships didn't bring Arne any cheer. Indeed, he could hardly bear even to think of ships. Mother tried to talk as usual, and so did Father, but no one's heart was in it.

Arne could not settle down to anything. He wanted to ask questions, but knew there could be no comforting answers. At last, without being told, he wandered off to bed.

It was hard for him to keep his mind on schoolwork the next morning. He rushed home at the midday recess, bolted his meal, got his field glasses, and went up to the cliff as fast as he could get there. Gustav's ship should be coming in soon, if it hadn't run into trouble. You never knew for sure when a freighter would be in. Father said it was always best to allow a little extra time even in good weather. But Arne had been hoping it might come in a little ahead of time. Perhaps he'd even catch sight of it today. Then there would certainly be rejoicing!

There was no sign of the ship as he looked out over the stormy waters, but he lingered so long on the cliff that he barely got into the schoolroom in time. Herr Engstrand looked at him severely, and though he said nothing, Arne realized he had better not cut it so close again.

He couldn't keep away from the cliff at noon. But each day he stood there, looking, only a short time and was careful to get to school before the bell rang.

At home, Mother was trying her best to keep everything normal, but she looked more and more anxious as the news of storms continued. Even Father, accustomed as he was to ships and storms at sea, looked anxious as he listened to the reports over the radio.

Christmas preparations went on, but there wasn't much laughing or singing over them now.

"Why don't we hear something?" Arne asked his father in desperation. "Couldn't they let someone know if they're in trouble? Couldn't help go to them?"

"We hear the names of some of the ships in trouble. But no word comes of the *Stjerne*," his father said, and paused. "I hope it is just that their radio has gone bad. Yes, that must be it." He spoke as if he wanted to reassure himself as much as Arne.

That day the bell had rung before Arne slid into his seat at school. He got a sharp reprimand from the teacher, but for once he didn't care. He could only think of Gustav, out there on the stormy sea.

But Bergel *did* care. She knew Christmas plans were afoot in school, and she could not bear to have him get into trouble now. The next noon Bergel was watching for her cousin, and when she saw him start toward the cliff, she seized her sled and ran after him.

64

"Arne! Arne!" she called over and over as she neared the cliff, but the wind was strong, and he did not hear her. She hurried on, faster than ever, looking anxious but determined. If they didn't look out, they'd both be late for school.

Yes, there he was, high up on the very peak of the cliff, looking out to sea through his field glasses. She called and shouted, waving her arm in a frantic signal. This time he heard, put his glasses away, and started down.

"Look here, Bergel, you didn't need to come—" he began, slightly annoyed.

"I know," interrupted Bergel. "But today I think Herr Professor is going to announce the trip up the mountain for Christmas greens. You don't want to be late and maybe have to stay home from that. I think my sled will get us there on time."

"So!" said Arne. Bergel was a pretty good kid. "Hop on, then. We'll beat that school bell. We'll take the short cut, shall we? That'll get us there all right."

"Well," said Bergel, hesitating a little. "It's dangerous, but—"

"Not with your cousin Arne as navigator! Come on!"

Arne was daring, Bergel knew that, but he was skillful, too. And she certainly didn't want to be late today.

Herr Professor might punish latecomers by refusing to let them go on that expedition up the mountain for the Christmas greens. She got on the sled and shut her eyes tight as they went flying down the steep hill toward the schoolgrounds. She was a little frightened, it is true, but almost too excited to realize it. If they avoided that big rock now, they'd be all right.

Arne's face was grim as they whizzed downward.

This was a dangerous hill. He had to give all his attention to steering and braking. Bergel had risked her own good record and the chance of going up the mountain in order to warn him. He just had to get her back safely and on time.

It was a triumphant moment when the breathless ride was accomplished safely, and the cousins jumped off the sled. Then they made a dash across the schoolground.

Arne's thoughts were racing as fast as his feet. Where was that ship, anyway? It was really overdue now, several days. Maybe something had happened to Captain Olsen. Maybe Gustav had to bring in the ship. What if he had had to take command and had failed to bring it safely to port? Arne couldn't bear to think of such a thing.

He looked so anxious that Bergel, glancing at him as they pulled off their coats, said softly, "Don't forget—it's the Christmas *Star* we're waiting for. And remember, that's always come in safe and sure."

Arne nodded and hurried across the schoolroom and slid into his seat just as the bell rang. His spirits, never down for very long, rose a little. He and Bergel had made port safely, anyhow, and in time, too.

But Herr Professor Engstrand looked at him gravely for a moment and said, "Tardiness is a fault I do not wish my pupils to develop. Arne Dalen, you have come in once this week just after the bell rang, and you have repeatedly got in barely on time. I shall have to take strong measures if you are tardy again."

Arne's face flushed, and he looked down in embarrassment. If he could only explain! But you couldn't explain things to Herr Professor.

He was heartily glad when the teacher went on in an entirely different tone, "I have a pleasant announcement to make. On Friday afternoon, all you older pupils are to go up the mountain for greens to decorate the schoolhouse for the Christmas program. All bring flashlights and sandwiches. We shall make a campfire and have a picnic. Froken Utvig promises we shall practice some of our Christmas songs there."

There was a stir of delight throughout the room. The trip up the mountain for Christmas greens was a favorite yearly event. Getting the greens and decorating was even more fun than the Christmas program itself. This was the first time Arne and Bergel's class had been included in the expedition. Arne's eyes glowed as he thought of the picnic supper, the campfire up there on the dark mountain, the singing that would float all up and down the mountainside.

But some of the girls looked a little perturbed, and the teacher almost smiled as he said, "We shall not stand out there in the snow eating our supper. Froken Utvig says we can find shelter in her father's saeter cabin."

The Utvig saeter! Oh, that would be something, Arne thought. Everyone said the Utvig cabin was the finest on the mountain. Arne had never been there, and he almost forgot about the *Stjerne* in his excitement. It was wonderful fun to go up to a saeter in summer, but in winter it would be a real adventure. He resolved to be on time for the rest of the week. He certainly could not run the chance of being left out of that trip up the mountain.

Arne could hardly keep his feet from taking the familiar cliff path the next noon. If only there were just a little daylight after school. Then he'd hurry as fast as he could up the cliff, get out those field glasses, and stand looking as long as he liked. But it would be dark by that time. And tomorrow was the day of the trip up the mountain. No, he couldn't run the risk of being late.

With a mighty effort he managed to trudge straight to school. He even got there a little early. He was too anxious and miserable to stay out playing, so he earned the pleased surprise of Herr Professor by going straight into the schoolroom, opening his book, and settling down.

69

But his thoughts were not on his Norwegian history, though that was a subject he really liked, full as it was of stirring events. His thoughts were with the freighter *Stjerne,* in peril out there on the stormy sea.

Arne hurried home right after school, hoping better news had come in. His mother was in a perfect fury of baking. She was making *lefse,* and he usually liked to watch her doing that. But today he didn't care much, for one look at her face told him that the news was not good.

She whisked the kettle of potatoes off the fire, mashed them violently, mixed in flour and salt and cream. Then she rolled out the dough into large, thin, round cakes, and Besta baked them on the top of the cookstove.

Both of them nodded a greeting to him, but no one seemed to feel like talking. Presently Besta buttered a piece of warm *lefse,* spread it with brown sugar, rolled it, and handed it to Arne. Even now he did not forget the polite Norwegian *"Mange tak,"* "Many thanks."

He took his *lefse* and wandered off to the workshop, but there was a lump in his throat as he drew the covering back and looked at his little ships. It didn't seem to him he could work at them today, and he started to cover them again. Then he stopped and said fiercely right out loud, "Look here, Arne Dalen! Gustav wouldn't do that. He's a great one to stick at something until he gets it done."

Somehow that idea comforted Arne. Wherever Gustav was, even if he was in serious difficulties, he'd be doing something to try to put things right. He remembered how quick and sure his brother had been last summer on the *Laks* when the rocks had fallen. And Gustav had weathered bad storms before this. Captain Olsen, too. They were two good men, Father said. And they had a good crew of Norwegian sailors. Arne picked up one of the little ships and began a careful job of sandpapering. Even after supper he came out and found comfort in working. When Gustav came home, the surprise would be ready.

He lingered in the kitchen next morning for a few minutes after the others had gone about their various duties. He wanted to talk to Mother about preparations for that trip up the mountain. But more than that, he wanted very much to say something encouraging to her.

It was hard to know just what to say. The Dalens came from a long line of seafaring people, and no one talked much about it when there were storms and ships were overdue. But Arne couldn't bear that bleak look on his mother's face. It was not at all like her. She was a cheerful, busy person, almost as full of lively plans and ideas as Arne himself.

71

It didn't take long to settle about the lunch. Mother promised to make him some extra nice *smörbröd,* or sandwiches. At a picnic like that, all the sandwiches would be spread out and shared, and hers must do both Arne and herself credit. She promised to decorate them in all kinds of fancy patterns. She would put in some of the *bakkelse,* too, and other cakes.

Arne was well pleased with this, but he didn't quite know how to go on to the next subject. Then Bergel's words of comfort came back to him. They had made him feel better. Maybe Mother would like them too. He cleared his throat and said gruffly, "Gustav's ship is the Christmas *Star,* you know, Mother. It'll come in safe, I'm just sure it will."

Tears sprang into his mother's eyes and brimmed over, and Arne wished earnestly that he had not spoken at all. He didn't know whether to keep still now or to try again, so he just put his arm around her and gave her a quick, fervent hug.

She swallowed hard, shook herself, and wiped her eyes fiercely. "There now, Arne," she said, hustling the dishes off the table. "Of course it will come in." And somehow she managed to smile. "Run to school now, boy. Don't be late."

When Arne came home at noon, a lunch was ready packed for him to take up the mountain. He got out his flashlight and skis and put all the things together. His mother tried to talk cheerfully of all these preparations as they ate their lunch, but her sentences trailed off in a way not at all like her.

The boy's heart was heavy as he left the house. He started for school, then stopped and swung swiftly around. He'd go like lightning up the cliff, and maybe he'd see Gustav's ship. Then he'd ski down the slope and tell his mother. He'd have time. He was starting back to school earlier than usual.

He hesitated just an instant. This was no day to be late. Then he set off at full speed toward the cliff.

He caught his breath in exultation as his glasses swept the angry, heaving waves. It was beginning to snow, but in spite of that he could see there was a ship far out—a ship that could be the *Stjerne!* But it was much too far away for him to make sure. And yet he couldn't bear to leave in uncertainty. The minutes flew by as he stood there, too intent on watching to think of anything else.

Suddenly a bell far down below brought him up with a jerk. That was the school bell. First bell, only. If he skied like mad, he might make it.

But though he felt as if he were actually flying down the slope, the last bell sounded loud and clear through the wintry air before he even reached the schoolground.

With all his heart Arne wished he didn't have to go into that schoolroom. But he knew he did. He paused for an instant at the door. Then he braced himself and entered, his head erect but his cheeks crimson as he walked quickly and quietly to his desk.

There was an air of excitement in the room, and Herr Engstrand had evidently been talking, for no books were open. Now he paused and waited till Arne took his seat.

"I am very sorry you chose to be late this noon, Arne," he said, and though his tone was stern, it did sound a little regretful, too. "I dislike very much to keep you in today of all days, but you have been warned and spoken to more than once. Get out your English grammar and do the exercises on pages 63 and 64. Have them on my desk before you leave the schoolroom. And now the rest of you may get your wraps and skis. As I was beginning to explain, it has been decided on account of the threatening snow that we start at once and get back before too late. The afternoon session is excused."

Arne sent a stunned glance at Bergel. They were actually going to have a half-holiday and go up the mountain. And they were leaving him out of it. Her face, sorrowful and reproachful, didn't make him feel any better. In the flurry of leaving, she seemed very busy with one or two papers. Then she gave him a long look and rose to go with the others.

6

As the other children trooped out, Arne pretended to be deep in his work. Let them go then, and have a good time. What did they care about his troubles? They didn't have a brother out on the stormy sea and a worried family at home. Let them go, and see if he cared! But he did care, tremendously. There was a lump in his throat he couldn't swallow.

Bergel passed his seat and touched his shoulder gently. He shrugged off her hand, but she slid it down toward his and left a piece of paper there. He acted as if he didn't see it, for he was hurt and disappointed and angry. Probably just a note saying he should have been more careful. He wouldn't even look at it.

The shouting and laughter died away at last, and Arne looked gloomily down at his books. He felt more like crying than doing exercises. But of course he was too big to do a thing like that. If only Herr Engstrand had given him anything but English grammar to do! He must know how Arne disliked that. Arithmetic, now—he could have got that done in a hurry and maybe he could have caught up with the others. But English grammar! And two long exercises! He'd never get those done.

Suddenly he remembered another trip up the mountain—the summer trip, when he had thought he would have to stay home to bale *lutfisk*. With Gustav's help, he had got that job done in time to go with the others. No one was here to help him now, but perhaps he could get this job done himself and follow the others. His usual hopefulness began to come to his rescue. Herr Engstrand hadn't said he couldn't come on the trip. He had only said he must finish the exercises before he left.

Arne turned to his books in earnest, now. He knew how to do that first sentence, anyway. Maybe this wasn't such a hard exercise, after all. He was half through it, his spirits rising as he worked, when his hopes fell again. He didn't know the way to the Utvig saeter, and he was well enough acquainted with mountains to realize that a snowy day in December was no time to strike out on unfamiliar ways.

He gave a deep sigh and turned back to his work. No use to try to get it done fast. It didn't matter when he finished. But he went doggedly on, and a sudden thought came to him. Bergel had certainly looked as if she wanted to tell him something. He picked up the note, his face brightening as he read: "Utvig saeter is above ours. Go up the Ahlness trail, then take the left fork where there are three saeter cabins." She had even scrawled a little map. With fresh energy, Arne bent to his lesson.

The schoolroom clock had ticked an hour away when the boy laid his exercises on Herr Professor's desk. He put on his skis, settled his knapsack on his back, and set off on his trip up the mountain through the falling snow.

The boy felt confident and light-hearted as he hastened up toward his uncle's saeter. Though the familiar landmarks looked different in their winter dress, he could recognize them without difficulty. He knew he was making better time alone than the others could in a large company. As he sped along he began to hope he might overtake them, or at least get there in time to help bring in the greens.

The snow, which fell heavily at first, began to slacken a little. He managed to go along at a steady pace, but it seemed a long time before he came out where Uncle Jens's cabin faced the fjord. The little log house looked forlorn with all its windows boarded over for winter, and Arne was anxious to hurry on. Far out at sea he could detect the faint light of a ship. He wondered if it could possibly be the *Stjerne.*

The snow had stopped now, and strong winds blew in steadily from the sea. Dusk had closed in, and Arne shivered as he stood there, not sure how to go ahead. "Take the Ahlness trail," Bergel's note had said. There was more than one path zigzagging about up here, he knew, but as far as he could remember, there was only one good trail that led way up the mountain. That must be the one. Those folks up there ahead must have left plenty of tracks. But he had difficulty in finding them because of the drifting snow. At last, however, with the aid of his flashlight, he did manage to find some traces.

If only Bergel had said how far it was! It seemed to Arne that the way was much longer than he had expected it to be. Though he got out his flashlight often, he didn't see anything of three saeter cabins in a cluster, to say nothing of a fork in the trail. The way was very steep in places, and he did wish those tracks were plainer.

And now he had come to a place where the snow was so drifted he couldn't see any tracks at all. He was uncertain what to do, which way to take, and almost wished he had never started on this difficult journey alone.

Then he looked up toward the mountain top, and just above it, where the wind had ripped the clouds apart, he saw one bright star shining. Christmas star again, thought Arne, and felt a little better. He pressed on and at last came to the three small houses. Now for the fork in the trail!

But he could not make out any tracks in the drifted snow, and there didn't seem to be any real trail, though there was a break in the bushes here. He'd start that way. But he hadn't gone far when he was brought up short by a great boulder in the way. This certainly could not be the trail. He went back and started again, but this time a thicket of bushes blocked the path. Perhaps, after all, he had come the wrong way. Perhaps those three cabins were not the ones Bergel had meant. His heart was thumping. What if he was lost in these mountains?

He stood there straining his eyes in the gray darkness. If only he could catch some gleam of the campfire! He could see no sign of light on the dark mountain, but as he stood, trying to think of something he could do, a familiar sound come down to him—a long-drawn blast that could only come from a saeter horn. Someone was certainly sending him a signal, and he felt sure it was Bergel.

Arne stood still, trying to determine just where that call had come from. As he waited, it came again, over and over. The star would be a good guide now, for the horn's blast had come from exactly that direction. Now, a little to the left, he found a way through the thicket; with the help of the horn and of his bright star, he forged steadily ahead.

At last, to his great relief and delight, he caught sight of a glimmer of light above him. Soon he began to hear voices in the distance—faint at first, then louder. Now he could hear calls and shouts and laughter and bits of song, and above all, the sound of the horn.

In a few moments the full brightness of the campfire burst upon him. He saw people scurrying about; but one small, valiant figure caught his eye and warmed his heart. It was Bergel, standing in the firelight, the long saeter horn at her lips. She blew a blast that Arne felt must be heard clear down at Nordheim, and he almost felt like giving her a hug. Instead he skied silently to her side and stood there grinning. "Calling someone, Bergel?" he asked.

"Arne!" she cried, and threw both arms around him. "Oh, I was so worried! I knew you'd try to come, and then it snowed so hard for a while, and drifted so, and you didn't know the way. How did you ever manage to find it?" Her tone showed plainly that she considered that quite a feat.

"Well, you helped," said Arne. He slipped away

from her embrace, but his voice was gentle. "And then I guess the Christmas star helped, too." He nodded to where the bright star shone among drifting clouds.

"You see! Isn't that a good sign?" said Bergel triumphantly. "And now you're in time to help with the greens, Arne. The boys have gone up there just a little ways. Got your hunting knife?"

"Do you suppose I'd come up here without it?" asked Arne. But he smiled at her, and she smiled back before she turned to help with the supper.

Everyone was glad to see Arne, though nobody said much about it. He pulled his silver-handled hunting knife from the sheath at his belt and was soon in the thick of the work, helping cut branches and put them in bundles.

In spite of himself, his respect for Herr Professor Engstrand increased as he watched him directing and helping. The teacher had obtained permission to take what they needed, and seemed to know exactly how to go about getting it. When he climbed easily up a big tree, Arne could hardly believe his eyes. Was this the same dignified man who didn't seem to be interested in anything but books and lessons and keeping order?

Eager to do his part now that he was here, Arne went right up to a treetop to get some specially fine branches with clusters of cones. When he came nimbly down, he saw, with some dismay, that the other boys had gone on and that only Herr Engstrand was at hand. He was probably in for a good scolding now, but surely Herr Professor wouldn't send him home when he had toiled so hard to get up here alone.

Arne started to run after the other boys, but the teacher took two or three long strides, laid a hand on his shoulder, and turned him around. "Just a minute, my boy," he said. "I have something to say to you."

Arne's heart seemed to go right down into his boots. "Yes, sir," he managed to mumble. "Maybe I shouldn't have come, but I—well, I did my exercises first, and I didn't think you said—" His voice trailed miserably off.

"I didn't say you shouldn't come," said the teacher in a matter-of-fact tone. "In fact, I hoped you would, though I didn't feel I could encourage you to do so, in view of the weather and the distance. Of course I know it takes more than a snowstorm to keep a Norwegian boy off a mountain. In fact, people say mountains and snow are all a Norwegian needs for fun. But I didn't think you knew the way here."

"I didn't really, but—" Arne began and then stopped short, uncertain and embarrassed. He certainly could not tell Herr Professor about Bergel's note. How could he explain?

Herr Engstrand was going on, "But your cousin told me—" He stopped so long that Arne looked up and, to his great surprise, saw that his teacher was smiling a little. "She is a conscientious little girl, as well as a good pupil, and I think she felt she might not have done right. And then, too, I think she began to get worried about you. So she told me about leaving you the note. And I'll admit we were all a little anxious when you did not arrive."

"Those grammar exercises," said Arne, with a gusty sigh. "They took quite a while. But who thought of the saeter horn? That was a life-saver."

"It was Bergel who thought of that, and Froken Utvig found it for her. Bergel told me something else, Arne. She told me why you had been late those times. I should have been glad if you had told me yourself."

"You would?" exclaimed Arne in astonishment, and added, with complete honesty, "I never thought of that."

Herr Engstrand dropped his hand from Arne's shoulder. "I see," was all he said, but his voice made Arne think of the way he himself sometimes felt when he tried very hard to do something and did not succeed.

That tone made Arne want to mend matters, and he

hurried on, "I didn't know you'd be interested, but I guess you are. So I want to tell you why I was late this noon. Bergel didn't know about that. I saw a ship way out in the storm and I thought it might be Gustav's. And from Uncle Jens's saeter I could still see the lights of a ship a good ways out."

"I see," Herr Engstrand said again. But this time his tone was quite different. "A ship would have a hard time making port in a sea like this."

Arne looked up at him in alarm. "Oh, Herr Professor Engstrand!" he exclaimed. "Do you suppose—what if Gustav's ship got nearly home only to be dashed to pieces on the rocks?"

"Of course the chances are it was not the *Stjerne* at all," said Herr Engstrand. His voice was thoughtful.

"Oh, I wish that wind would go down," said Arne fervently. "There aren't even any stars out, now."

"Well, Arne, these Norwegian skippers know our coast pretty well, don't forget that. And from what I hear, Captain Olsen is a fine navigator. Come, Bergel is blowing the horn again. That is the signal for supper."

Arne gathered with the others around the great fire piled high in the kitchen fireplace. Froken Utvig and the girls had scrubbed a long table, laid a bright cloth over it, and spread it with gaily-decorated sandwiches and cakes. Everyone was hungry and ready for the good food and the singing.

There were Christmas songs first, and folk songs followed. Then everyone stood to sing the national anthem:

"Yes, we love with fond devotion
Norway's mountain domes,
Rising storm-lashed o'er the ocean
With their thousand homes."

"'Storm-lashed' is right," thought Arne. But he loved the fine old anthem, just as the others did, and joined in the singing with all his heart.

"I think those songs all but lifted the roof," said Froken Utvig, smiling. "But now, as it is still snowy and drifting, and the wind is strong, we had better start home."

Everyone hurried about—putting out the fire, getting things in order. Arne was as busy as anyone, but he couldn't help thinking about the *Stjerne*. What if she was tossing about out there, very close to the rocky shore, driven by the wind? What if Gustav should be almost in port, only to have his ship go down tonight?

His face was troubled as he bent to fasten his skis, but he looked up quickly as Herr Professor came over

87

to him and said, "Arne, I want you to help me with some of these greens. Can you carry a load as big as this, do you think? We'll fasten it on your back if you can."

Ordinarily Arne would have been proud of such a request, for the load was a large one. But tonight he had planned to rush ahead with all speed and see if it could be possible that his brother's ship had come in. He couldn't make much time with such a load. But he could do nothing but answer, "Yes, sir, I can."

"Good boy," said Herr Engstrand. "Now, Arne, I want you to stay behind with me just a little. I have one or two things to do."

"Yes, sir," said Arne, but his disappointment showed so plainly that Herr Professor said, "What is it, boy?"

"It's my brother's ship, sir," said Arne, in a low tone. "I thought she might have come in. I wanted to—"

"Yes, yes, I see. Well, Arne, that's why I want you to stay behind. An idea has occurred to me—a way you and I may be able to help your brother. I have told Froken Utvig to let some of the big boys guide the party."

"Yes, sir," said Arne again, but this time he was thoroughly puzzled. How could he and Herr Engstrand up here on the mountain possibly be of any help to Gustav out there on the stormy sea?

7

THERE WAS a good deal of laughter as the boys divided the greens and arranged the loads on their backs. Then away they went, singing and shouting, the girls insisting on carrying some of the smaller branches with especially fine cones.

How Arne wished that he could be a member of the merry group! He wanted to get down to Nordheim fast, and it seemed to him that Herr Engstrand was taking a good deal of time over things that were not necessary.

But once the others were out of sight, the teacher said, "Now, Arne, full speed ahead down to your uncle's saeter. The wind is getting higher. It feels to me as if it's going to snow again, and we've got work to do, you and I."

Arne was more puzzled than ever. What work could they possibly have to do up here? But Herr Engstrand was skiing down the mountain with a speed that Arne found hard to follow. When he reached Uncle Jens's saeter, Herr Engstrand was already there, playing his flashlight all around the little clearing.

From the high point near the cliff, the boy could see lights moving out on the open sea leading to the fjord. "Looks as if a ship's in trouble out there," he said anxiously. "Are we going on down, sir?"

"No, here's where we stop, Arne. Let us make a big fire, you and I, and keep it going to give a signal to that ship. They can tell from the height that this is the cliff, and if I'm not mistaken, they'll know the harbor is below here."

"Oh, that's the plan!" exclaimed Arne. It was such a good one, and yet so simple, he wondered why he hadn't thought of it himself. Neither of them said much; but they worked fast, and a fire was soon started near the edge of the cliff.

"Now, Arne," said Herr Engstrand, "we will pile our boughs on this and make a big blaze right away while we collect more."

"So that's why you wanted me to take such a big load!" said Arne. "And you took a lot more than I did, even."

"I wanted to get this thing going right away. There!" He threw his bundle on the fire. "Pitch yours on, Arne."

Arne threw his pine boughs on and watched with satisfaction as they burst into a great blaze.

"Now we must collect plenty of fuel, Arne. I have my small hatchet, of course. And you have your hunting knife. We must keep this fire burning high and bright. Then we'll watch to see what happens out there."

Arne did a good deal of thinking as he dragged in branches and twigs. This wasn't a bit like the Herr Professor who had been so stern and strict and had seemed interested only in lessons. This was really smart—like something Gustav himself might have thought of. He'd like to tell Herr Professor so, but even now he could not quite get up his courage to do that. But when they had collected a large pile of wood and were standing by the fire watching those lights out at sea, he did manage to ask, "Herr Professor, how did you happen to think of doing this?"

"Well, Arne, I was a commando in the war," Herr Engstrand said quietly.

"A commando!" gasped Arne.

"Yes. We learned to think of all sorts of ways to do

things in emergencies. More than once we guided a vessel safely to port just this way."

"A commando! That's what Gustav wanted to be. But he wasn't quite old enough. He says they learned everything, just about."

"Well, we did learn a lot of things. For one thing, we learned to obey orders fast and to the letter." He paused for a moment and went on, more as if he were thinking aloud than speaking to his companion, "But schoolboys aren't commandos, and I don't suppose you can expect—" He broke off and looked at Arne with a quizzical expression.

Arne was standing very straight, his eyes eager and alert as he looked back at Herr Engstrand. "Oh, sir, but I think you can expect us to—" He stopped as if he had just remembered something. "From now on," he said emphatically, "I'm sure you can expect that."

"I believe I can, Arne," said Herr Professor.

His voice was serious; but it was friendly, too, and now Arne did not find it very hard to muster courage to say, "All the boys would like to know about your being a commando. The girls, too. Couldn't you—wouldn't you tell them about that? We'd all be interested."

"You would?" In the firelight, Arne could see that

his teacher was smiling a little. "I had an idea school was for lessons. But maybe there are several kinds of lessons. And now, Arne, up and at 'em. More wood!"

Arne rushed off, but this time he had new hope. He was working with a commando! And the commandos had got out of all sorts of dangerous situations. Herr Engstrand seemed confident that Captain Olsen and Gustav would do the same thing and bring the *Stjerne* in safely.

Each time they returned to the fire, they stopped to watch the ship struggling out there against the wind. Then they dashed back to work harder than ever. It was not easy to collect enough fuel in the snow, but both of them worked with a will.

At last Arne said hopefully, "I think she's making progress out there, sir."

"Yes, looks as if she's making for the channel. Come on, Arne. We have to keep the fire high and bright now."

When they returned the next time, Arne gave a great shout. "She's coming in! She's coming in! Oh, if she can just hold her course, she'll be safe."

"Yes, she's making headway all right. Looks as if it could be the *Stjerne,* Arne."

Arne fairly flew off to get more wood, his heart beating so hard he couldn't even talk. This time, when they came back to the fire, there was no doubt about it. "She's past the barrier now, and moving into the channel," said Herr Professor.

"Oh, Herr Professor!" Arne shouted, and in his exuberance he snatched off his cap and threw it so high it almost came down in the fire. "It's Gustav's ship! It's Gustav's ship, safe and sound. I know it is."

"How would you like to start down, Arne, and be there on the dock to greet your brother? Everybody will be there, and I know you'd like to be on hand with the others."

"Oh, boy!" cried Arne joyfully. "Oh, boy!" But then he looked quickly at the teacher. "But we couldn't leave the fire, could we? They still need it, don't they? This is about as important a time as any, isn't it?"

"Yes, we have to keep it going till we're sure they're safe. But I could manage to tend it alone now, if you'd like to get started down."

Arne hesitated just a moment. He wanted dreadfully to be right down there on the dock when the *Stjerne* came in. But then he shook his head. "No," he said. "One commando would never walk out on another. I'm going to help keep this fire going."

"Good boy, Arne. I think your brother would like that," said Herr Professor. There was an expression of such approval and pleasure on his face that Arne's cheeks flamed and he looked away, feeling very happy. "We'll both work hard, then; and we're pretty fast on our skis. We'll go down a lot faster than we came up. The ship won't beat us in by much."

In the very midst of gathering his next load of wood, Arne stopped and laughed right out loud. "I've thought of something, Herr Professor!" he cried. "I've thought of how I can get down there fast—just like a commando. We can keep the fire going as long as necessary, and I can still beat the ship to the dock."

"And how are you going to do that, Arne?"

"I can go right down the wires Uncle Jens arranged to let the milk and stuff down the cliff. Gustav did that last summer when he saw Torger Blessom's boat over-turned." He hesitated a moment. "I was wishing then I had the nerve to do it."

"And now you have!" said Herr Professor with a nod. "You'll need rope for that, Arne."

"Yes, there's one up here. I know where it's kept. And can't we sort of bundle me up in greens, a little?"

"Yes, and you'll need something more than mittens
95

to put on your hands to keep them from getting cut."

"Yes, Gustav wound a lot of cloth around his, I remember that. And I know where Aunt Tina keeps some rags we can use. One good thing—there's plenty of snow at the foot of the cliff; so I should make a good landing."

Herr Engstrand laughed. "Arne, I see plainly you've got the makings of a first-rate commando!" he said. "You've got good Viking blood. Your brother is going to be proud of you. We'll send you right down those wires to welcome him, all right."

"She's coming in! She's coming in, Herr Professor! Here she comes, the Christmas *Star!* She doesn't look very big, way down there!"

"No, we usually think of a Christmas star high above us in the heavens, instead of far below us on the water," said Herr Professor.

"I guess a Christmas star isn't out of place anywhere, is it?" said Arne. "The *Stjerne* is sure going to look good to us in that harbor. We won't need to bring in many more loads now, will we?"

The fire on the cliff blazed high, and the two worked fast to keep it replenished. The ship came closer and closer to port; and at last Herr Engstrand said, "They don't need our fire any more, Arne. The lights of the town will be enough. Now we'll get you ready, and down you go!"

Both of them worked fast to get Arne ready for his journey down. Herr Engstrand made sure the rope was safe and strong before he tied the loop in which Arne was to sit. Soon the boy was bundled up in greens, his hands well wrapped. Herr Professor settled him securely in the rope sling.

"I'll hold as tight as I can at first," he said. "But once you get going, you'll have a fast ride. Ready now? Here you go, down the wires to meet the Christmas *Star!*"

"Ready!" Arne managed to say, but his mouth was dry, and when he tried to swallow it seemed to him his heart was right up in his throat. The lights of Nordheim looked far, far below him.

Then Herr Professor gave him a little push and started him downward. Arne knew his teacher was holding the rope as firmly as possible, but the sling went in jerks along the wires. Probably they were rusty. What if they should break? The rope, too! It had been used all summer long. It might be a little frayed. What if it should break, with all this jerking?

Then he remembered how Gustav had thrown his

97

weight first one way and then another to steady his progress. He tried to do the same now, and he began to go faster and more smoothly.

Once fairly started, it was a swift, breathless ride Arne had down those wires. Fast as he was used to going on skis and sleds, he had never had such a ride as this. The blood pounded in his ears as he rushed through the air toward the foot of the cliff.

He hoped fervently that there would be a good, deep snowdrift where he landed. There was! In another instant, Arne, encased in greens, his hands bound with rags, plumped right into the midst of a great drift.

He heard the deep, throaty blast of the ship and a loud cheer from the people who had gathered on the dock. He struggled and pushed, trying to get free. After all he had gone through, here he was stuck in a drift. And the *Stjerne* was almost in port.

8

Arne managed to struggle out of the snowdrift at last, and to get free of the rope, but even then he could not rid himself of the greens nor the rags so firmly tied about his hands. But he was determined not to miss meeting that ship, even if he had to roll all the way to the dock. Once he got there, someone would help him out of his strange trimmings. What if he did look like a combination snowdrift and walking Christmas tree?

It was Bergel who saw him coming. She gave a scream of alarm and then burst into laughter as Arne shouted, "It's just me—Arne!"

She flew to his rescue, and Mother hurried to him too, and Margret and Besta. He soon stood free of his greens and rags, explaining a little in quick, eager sentences. But there was scant time for explanation, for the *Stjerne's* bells were ringing, her whistle was blowing, and she was in port.

All of them rushed to be right there when Gustav came down the gangplank. Then there was excitement and joy, talk and laughter, and even happy tears.

"I want to hear everything, Gustav—what happened—tell us all about it!" cried Arne, rushing at his brother.

"Wait now," said his mother. "Gustav, we have such a supper for you! Uncle Jens and all are coming over. It is enough now we have you safe home. We will hear the story at supper."

What a story Gustav had to tell—a story of storms, of a ship for a time fairly sheeted with ice. He told of the injury to the engines, of the radio going bad, of a struggling trip home, then another storm when they were almost there.

"It was a big fire on the cliff that helped us—perhaps really saved us," he said. "We were trying to stay away from shore, the winds out there were so violent. Then this fire guided us in. I wonder who made that fire."

"Arne did that," said Bergel proudly. "Arne and Herr Professor Engstrand."

"Of course it was his idea," Arne said modestly. And the little company listened in wonder as he explained how Herr Engstrand had thought of the plan and they had worked together to carry it out.

"That was smart, Arne, really smart!" said Gustav. "I want to know this Herr Professor of yours. He must have had confidence in you, too, to have you help like that. It was a big job, and a good one."

Arne hadn't thought of that idea, and it pleased him enormously.

"Do you like our Herr Engstrand better now, Arne?" asked Bergel.

"Like him!" cried Arne. "A commando like that—someone who knew just the right thing to do? Of course I like him. Not many boys have such a teacher!"

His mother smiled at him. She had a feeling there wouldn't be much trouble about school from now on. "I think we must ask Herr Professor here to share our Christmas Eve," she said. "I believe he is far from his home."

Christmas preparations were redoubled now. There were only a few days left, and work had lagged a little of late. Mother and Besta and Margret cleaned and baked and cooked from morning till night.

Arne was very thankful he had stuck at his shipmaking in spite of everything. Those ships would all be ready in time. He had only a little more painting to finish. His big problem now was how to get them on the Christmas tree without having everyone find out about them.

Mother and Besta and Margret always trimmed the tree. It stood in the best room; the door was shut, and Mother kept her eye on it. Arne certainly didn't see how he was going to get those ships hung.

This year Uncle Jens's family was to share Christmas Eve with them. Arne knew Signe and Bergel were bringing some new tree ornaments they had made—little straw goats, such as *Julenissen* was supposed to ride.

These would be entrusted to Mother. But Arne couldn't do that with his ships. They were to be a surprise for everyone.

The night before Christmas Eve he was still turning the problem over in his mind when he went to bed, and he stayed awake at least ten minutes, thinking it over. When he awoke the next morning, the solution had come to him. It was so simple he laughed out loud. He should have thought of that right away. He would take Gustav into his confidence, and after the tree was trimmed they would somehow smuggle in the little ships and hang them all over the tree.

Gustav agreed readily to this plan. "Say, I want to see those ships," he said, and to Arne's pleasure insisted on going out to the workshop then and there. "These are good, Arne," he said, picking up one and another. "Really good."

Arne was pleased yet a little shy, too, at the praise. "I did them mostly for you," he said, "and when you were so late coming it was awfully hard to keep at them."

Gustav nodded. "I can believe that all right, boy, but I'm glad you stuck," he said, and his dark eyes were softer than usual. "You practically built Norway a new merchant fleet here."

"Now how are we going to get them in there, Gustav?" asked Arne.

"We'll smuggle them in while the womenfolk are busy about supper. You'll have them all bundled up ready, won't you? We may have to make a foray in through the parlor window."

"Commando raid!" said Arne with a grin.

Gustav grinned back and rumpled Arne's hair so that it stuck up even more than usual. "That's right. And on defenseless womenfolk at that. Now I'd say late this afternoon would be about right. How does that strike you?"

Arne chuckled. "About the time Father fires off the gun that tells us it's Christmas Eve. You and I will be putting up the sheaves of grain for the birds, and it will give us a good chance to get away."

"You've got the idea, boy! And there's lots to do between then and now."

There was plenty to do indeed. Mother was calling Arne even as he came out of the workshop. She had many errands for him, but her voice was so happy Arne felt he wouldn't mind running his legs off. Anyway, Christmas errands were always fun.

There were baskets of good things to be carried to

half a dozen houses. Mother delighted especially in remembering anyone less fortunate than themselves at Christmas time. And Arne went with Father to get the smoked and pickled herring that was a favorite part of the *koltbord* feast.

It was fun, too, to dash in and out of the kitchen where mutton was roasting for the Christmas Eve supper, where the *lutfisk* was soaking ready to be simmered and drenched with butter, where everything was in the most delightful bustle of preparation.

But whatever he was doing, his mind was not far from those ships he must get ready to smuggle into the parlor. It was well into the afternoon before he could find an opportunity to get out to the workshop. He worked fast yet carefully, grinning to himself as he bundled up the little ships.

Gustav was busy with affairs of his own, back and forth to the dock many times. Once Arne saw him whisk around the corner of the house with a large crated affair that made the boy's hopes go way up. Could it be possible that the *Stjerne* had brought him his longed-for bicycle? That might mean he could take a holiday jaunt next summer, up the fjords and through the mountain valleys with some of the other boys. Herr Professor Engstrand was

105

planning to conduct such a trip, he knew, and wouldn't it be wonderful if he could go along?

His work was done now, and a good thing, too, for Mother was calling him to scrub himself thoroughly and get into his new Christmas clothes.

He was just ready when it was time for Father to fire that Christmas salute. Then Gustav was calling him, and together they went to the barn to get the two sheaves of grain that were ready to be put up on poles for the birds. To Arne's annoyance, Margret for once insisted on helping with that. She ought to know it was men's work. Perhaps it was because she was so glad to have Gustav safe home that she wanted to be with him more than usual. Arne looked at his brother in despair. How could they manage about those ships if Margret stuck with them?

But he could see Gustav wasn't worried, just amused; so he dropped his own worries and enjoyed the little ceremony as much as the others did.

"I think Mother's looking for you, Margret," said Gustav, when the birds were swooping down on their feast. Margret picked up her full holiday skirts and ran to the house, while Gustav winked at Arne.

"It was all right, Arne. I did see Mother looking out and beckoning," he said, as they hurried off to the workshop. "Now, boy, we work fast. You've got the bundle ready, I see. Good!"

In a twinkling he was around the house, Arne at his heels, and through the parlor window, taking care not to muss those stiff white curtains. Without a word he brought out a very small pocket flashlight, and Arne had hard work not to giggle as they hung the little ships all around the tree.

It was done so fast that Arne could hardly believe they had finished the job, but in another moment they were safely around the corner of the house and sauntering in at the kitchen door.

"Just in time," said Besta. "Light the candles, you two. I see the folks coming, Herr Engstrand from one direction and Uncle Jens and his family from the other."

Soon the Christmas greeting of *"God Jul"* sounded through the house, and the guests assembled at that bountiful Christmas Eve table.

Christmas Eve supper was a wonderful meal, but Arne and Bergel could hardly wait for the parlor doors to open. Bergel was thinking of the straw goats she had helped Signe make, and Arne was anxious to hear what the others would say when they saw the boats. Perhaps some of them found it almost as hard to wait as Bergel

107

and Arne did. When little Knut slipped down from the table and went straight to that mysterious door, Mother and Father rose from the table.

That was the signal for everybody to stand up. Father went over to throw the door open.

There stood the tree in the lovely glow of candlelight —straw goats, ships, and all.

Arne was sure they had never had a prettier tree. There were all sorts of delighted comments. But Mother said, "Why, look at those ships! Where did those lovely things come from? Did you bring them, Gustav?"

"Arne's the lad who gets the credit for those. He made them all by himself—one for every person here, from Knut up. How's that for a good surprise!"

Arne stood there, his cheeks red, his eyes shining. No one could quite believe he had done it, and everyone was even more surprised than he had hoped.

"That took patience as well as skill," said Herr Eng-strand. And perhaps that quiet comment was the one that pleased Arne most of all.

The straw goats were admired, too, and the other ornaments the girls had made. Then it was time for the gifts.

There was a beautiful hand-knit blue and red

sweater for Arne, with mittens to match and fine socks for skiing. But when Father trundled a bicycle out from behind the tree straight toward him, Arne could hardly see anything else.

Bergel was exclaiming in delight over a small and lovely tea set. And all the others were just as pleased with their gifts.

In the excitement, Gustav went quietly out of the room, and even Arne did not notice him. He was eagerly examining his bicycle, turning the wheels, feeling the pedals, noting every detail of handlebar and seat, headlight and horn and luggage carrier.

"Herr Professor, do you think I might be big enough to go on that trip you're going to conduct next summer?" he asked eagerly. "Now that I have my bicycle?"

"You're big enough to suit me. But let's see what your father says."

"We will wait to hear what *Julenissen* says," answered Herr Dalen, his eyes twinkling. "If he seems to think you're a good boy—" He broke off as a great noise was heard in the hallway and a pair of astonishing figures burst in.

Everyone laughed and clapped, for here was *Julenissen* himself, with his pointed red cap and long whiskers.

109

He was larger than *Julenissen* really should be, for his feet touched the ground as he bestrode the straw-trimmed goat, *Julebuken*. But no one minded that, and everyone screamed and laughed and tried to get out of his way.

There seemed to be no bad children in the Dalen relationship, for *Julebuken* stamped about the room without bumping anyone. He went so fast, *Julenissen* had hard work to keep up with him, and soon the lively pair

were on their way again, *Julenissen* explaining, in a voice very like Gustav's, that this was a busy night.

"I didn't get bumped, Father!" cried Arne.

"Must be *Julenissen* thinks you are a good boy, then," said his father gravely, though his eyes twinkled. "I guess that means there's a summer trip ahead for you, Arne."

And now Mother and Besta brought out the special treat of Yule porridge—a delicate rice pudding made

with spices and milk. Gustav, his hair somewhat rumpled, was there eating with the others.

"We mustn't forget the bowl for *Julenissen*," said Arne, with a sidewise grin at his brother.

"No, he likes that," said Gustav soberly, and took another helping.

There would be Christmas songs and games to follow, but first Father read the Christmas story. At the beginning, Arne's mind was so full of his bicycle he could scarcely pay attention. But then a few of the beautiful, familiar words caught his ear.

"'When they saw the star, they rejoiced with exceeding great joy,'" Father was reading.

Why, that's exactly what they had done, right up here in Nordheim.

Arne thought of the star that had helped guide him to safety on the mountain. And he remembered what Bergel had said when he was so worried about Gustav. "The Christmas *Star* has always come in safe and sure," she had said.

Why, of course. The Christmas star was always safe and sure. And wherever you saw it, it brought "exceeding great joy." Arne drew a sigh of deep content and settled to listen. This was really Christmas.

112